FLUFFY
STRIKES BACK

A P.U.R.S.T. ADVENTURE

KIDS CAN PRESS

TO ROD, GLORIA AND SHANE, MY OTHER FAMILY

Text and illustrations © 2016 Ashley Spires

Kids Can Press gratefully acknowledges the financial support of the Government of Ontario, through the Ontario Media Development Corporation; the Ontario Arts Council; the Canada Council for the Arts; and the Government of Canada, through the CBF, for our publishing activity.

Published in Canada and the U.S. by Kids Can Press Ltd.
25 Dockside Drive, Toronto, ON M5A 0B5

Kids Can Press is a Corus Entertainment Inc. company

www.kidscanpress.com

The artwork in this book was rendered in Photoshop, under constant threat of alien attack.
The text is set in Fontoon.

Edited by Yasemin Uçar
Designed by Julia Naimska

Printed and bound in Shenzhen, China, in 6/2016 by C & C Offset

CM 16 0 9 8 7 6 5 4 3 2

J-GN
P.U.R.S.T ADVENTURE
444-1948

Library and Archives Canada Cataloguing in Publication

Spires, Ashley, 1978–, author, illustrator
      Fluffy strikes back / written and illustrated by Ashley Spires.
(A P.U.R.S.T. adventure)

ISBN 978-1-77138-127-7 (bound) — ISBN 978-1-77138-133-8 (pbk.)

      I. Title.

PS8637.P57F58 2016   jC813'.6   C2015-903113-3

SOME NAMES HAVE BEEN CHANGED
TO PROTECT THE IDENTITIES OF
PETS WHO APPEAR IN THIS BOOK.
ANY SIMILARITIES TO ACTUAL
EVENTS ARE PROBABLY BECAUSE
THIS ACTUALLY HAPPENED.

VRRRRRRRR

SHVRRRRRRM

SHVRRRRRRM

SHVRRRRRRRM

SHVRRRRMPT!

bzzzzz

bzzzzzzzz

bzzz

bzz

GOING DOWN ...

JUST ANOTHER DAY AT THE OFFICE.

LEVEL ONE: ADVANCED TACTICAL TRAINING

A LOT OF CATS DREAM OF HAVING THEIR OWN SPACE STATION ...

LEVEL TWO: RESEARCH AND DEVELOPMENT

LEVEL FIVE: EXECUTIVE COMMAND

BUT NOT ALL CATS CAN LIVE THAT LIFE.

SOMEONE HAS TO ORGANIZE THE TROOPS.

SOMEONE HAS TO ASSIGN SPACE STATIONS.

SOMEONE HAS TO BE IN CHARGE OF P.U.R.S.T.

AND THAT SOMEONE IS SERGEANT FLUFFY VANDERMERE.

FLUFFY CAN'T HAVE ANY DISTRACTIONS.

ploomp

CLASSIFIED

PLOMP!

HIS JOB IS TO PROTECT THE WORLD FROM ALIEN DOMINATION.

THE **WHOLE PLANET** IS FLUFFY'S SPACE STATION.

ALL THE PEOPLE IN THE WORLD ARE **HIS** HUMANS.

AND EVERY SPACE PET OUT THERE IS **HIS** RESPONSIBILITY.

OF COURSE, EVERY GOOD LEADER NEEDS A RIGHT-HAND CAT ...

AND THAT'S WHERE CLICK COMES IN. SHE'S HIS EYES AND EARS.

SHE MONITORS ALL OF P.U.R.S.T. BUSINESS ...

AND RELAYS ALL IMPORTANT INFORMATION TO THE SERGEANT.

FROM P.U.R.S.T. COMMAND CENTER ...

THEY WATCH OVER FLUFFY'S HIGHLY SKILLED OPERATIVES ...

OVERSEE EVERY SECRET OPERATION ...

AND ANALYZE ALIEN INTELLIGENCE.

THAT'S HOW THEY KNOW THAT LAST WEEK, COMMANDER
TOE-TOES NEUTRALIZED AN ALIEN COLONY ...

THAT ON TUESDAY, CAPTAIN POPCORN SAVED
THREE HUMANS FROM AN ALIEN ATTACK ...

AND THAT YESTERDAY, THE LONG-LOST PROFESSOR WAS RESCUED
FROM EVIL ALIEN CLUTCHES BY THE SENTINAL PARKWAY TEAM.

FLUFFY TAKES HIS JOB VERY SERIOUSLY.

THE LEADER OF P.U.R.S.T. HAS DEVOTED HIS LIFE TO HIS MISSION ...

TO KEEP SPACE PETS — AND THE WORLD — SAFE.

AND FLUFFY DOES **ALL THIS** WITHOUT EVER LEAVING HIS OFFICE.

HE WASN'T ALWAYS BEHIND A DESK.

HE WAS ONCE A SKILLED OPERATIVE OF P.U.R.S.T. HIMSELF.

HE WENT FROM FIGHTING ALIENS ON THE FRONT LINES ...

TO TRAINING THE NEXT GENERATION OF RECRUITS ...

TO SITTING AT A DESK, CALLING ALL THE SHOTS.

HE CAN HARDLY REMEMBER
THE EXCITEMENT OF BATTLING
REAL ALIENS WITH HIS
BARE PAWS.

BUT LIVING IN THE SAFEST, MOST SECURE BUILDING
IN THE WORLD CAN MAKE A CAT KIND OF LAZY.

IT'S THE EMERGENCY LINE!

CALL ANSWERED

ra-woof!

ruffa ...

woof!

AGENT GORDON HAS PICKED UP WORD OF AN UPCOMING ATTACK.

HE WAS UNABLE TO DECIPHER THE LOCATION ...

BUT HE CAN CONFIRM IT'S HAPPENING TODAY!

21

THIS MUST BE SERIOUS.

WHY WOULD THE INFORMANT COME ALL THIS WAY?

WHY NOT JUST SEND IN A REPORT AS USUAL?

WHAT COULD BE SO URGENT THAT SHE COULDN'T STOP FOR A WASH FIRST?

me ... eo ... ORRR!

slosh

IT'S A WARNING — THEY'RE COMING!

23

FINE TIME FOR A NAP.

LET HER SLEEP IT OFF WHILE THE SERGEANT THINKS THIS OVER.

THEY'RE COMING? WHO'S COMING? COMING WHERE?

HOW CAN FLUFFY POSSIBLY THINK IN THE MIDDLE OF THIS RACKET?

CAN'T SOMEONE SHUT THAT THING UP?

BLURM! BLURM! BLURM!

BLURM!

WAIT — IT'S THE ALARM.

BLURM!

clicka-clacka

BUT FLUFFY DIDN'T APPROVE A DRILL TODAY.

bzzzzz

FEED LOST

SECURITY CAMERA 1

SECURITY CAMERA 1

P.U.R.S.T. HEADQUARTERS IS UNDER ALIEN ATTACK!

zoooom!

GASP!

bzzzz   bzzz

sssvloooossshhh!

svlooosh!

WOOOOSH!

sssvlooosssshhh!

AND HE'S NOT GOING TO LET THEM GET HIS
SECOND IN COMMAND EITHER.

FLUFFY HAS TO BE SURE THE ALIENS CAN'T FOLLOW THEM.

CLICK IS IN SHOCK. NO ONE EVER TOLD HER ABOUT THE SECRET PASSAGE.

AND SHE HAS NEVER SEEN THIS SIDE OF FLUFFY BEFORE.

A SECRET BUNKER.

NO ONE BUT FLUFFY AND HIS ENGINEER, DARRYL, KNOW ABOUT IT.

KEEPING IT SECRET WAS A MATTER OF SECURITY.

AND RIGHT NOW, HE IS **VERY GLAD** HE KEPT THAT SECRET
ALL THESE YEARS.

THE SITUATION IS WORSE THAN THEY THOUGHT.

THE ALIENS ARE EVERYWHERE!

34

THEY'VE TAKEN HOSTAGES!

AND THEY'RE TORTURING THEM!

THEY'LL NEED A PLAN.

sandbox entrance

elevator

Level one

Level two

Level three

cadets held here

Level four

secret bunker

Level five

secret passage

THE MOST IMPORTANT THING WILL BE TO FREE THE HOSTAGES.

SINCE HE BARRICADED THE ENTRANCE TO THE BUNKER ...

FLUFFY HAS NO CHOICE BUT TO ENTER THROUGH THE SANDBOX.

DARRYL WILL HELP HIM GET TO THE SURFACE,
THEN RETURN TO HIS POST.

THEN FLUFFY WILL CLEAR EACH FLOOR TO MAKE SURE THAT
NO ALIENS CAN ATTACK FROM BEHIND.

HE WILL, OF COURSE, NEED TO PROTECT HIMSELF.

CLICK WON'T BE JOINING HIM THIS TIME.

HE WON'T PUT HER IN THAT KIND OF DANGER.

THIS WILL BE A SOLO MISSION.

P.U.R.S.T. IS HIS RESPONSIBILITY.

THOSE ARE HIS SPACE PETS.

THIS IS **HIS** FIGHT.

BESIDES, HE'LL NEED CLICK AND DARRYL TO STAY BEHIND AS LOOKOUTS.

THAT'S AN ORDER.

Meow!

Meow!

THEY CAN COMMUNICATE IF ANYTHING GOES WRONG.

AFTER ALL THESE QUIET YEARS, SERGEANT FLUFFY
VANDERMERE IS A CAT OF ACTION ONCE MORE.

TIME TO GET DOWN TO BUSINESS.

SPEAKING OF BUSINESS ...

VRRRRRRRR

SCRITCH

CLICK!

IT'S TIME TO TAKE BACK P.U.R.S.T.

SVRRRRRRM

SVRRRRRRM

SHVRRRMPT!

The text "47" appears at the bottom right as a page number.

FLUFFY WAS HOPING FOR A BIGGER CHALLENGE.

HE SHOULD BE CAREFUL WHAT HE WISHES FOR.

BZZZZZ!

BZZZZT!

THWAP! BZZZZT!

THUNK!

THAT WILL TEACH THEM.

BRRZZZ!

TAKE ON SERGEANT FLUFFY VANDERMERE AND YOU'LL
FIND YOURSELF IN A STICKY SITUATION.

HE'LL HAVE TO FIND ANOTHER WAY TO THE CADETS.

HE'S BEEN HIT!

BUT HE HAS TO KEEP MOVING.

NO ONE KNOWS P.U.R.S.T. HEADQUARTERS LIKE FLUFFY.

ONE FOR THEM ...

bzzzzzzz

fooosh

AND ONE FOR THEM.

HACKZZ!

GACKZZ!

ACKZZ!

YUP, EVEN AFTER ALL THESE YEARS ...

WOOOSH

gackz!

KATHUNK

FLUFFY'S STILL GOT IT.

plink

plink

bzzzz

bzzzz

BUZZZ!

GAH-ASP!

HAIRBALL ON A HOTPLATE!

CLASSIFIED

DON'T LOOK!

THEY HAVE THE SPACE PET MASTER FILE!

THAT'S WHAT THE ATTACK WAS ALL ABOUT!

THE ALIENS WANT TO STEAL THE NAMES AND LOCATIONS ...

OF EVERY SPACE PET AND SPACE STATION IN THE WORLD.

WITH THAT KNOWLEDGE, ALIENS COULD WIPE OUT P.U.R.S.T. FOREVER!

THERE IS NO WAY THEY ARE GETTING OUT OF HERE
WITH TOP-SECRET INFORMATION.

THEY MIGHT BE AN ANGRY SWARM ...

BUT THEY ARE NO MATCH FOR FLUFFY AND THE AGENTS OF P.U.R.S.T.

NICE TRY, BUT NO ONE CAN DEFEAT P.U.R.S.T.

P.U.R.S.T. HEADQUARTERS IS SECURE.

HE NOTIFIES CLICK AND DARRYL.

CLICK? DARRYL? NO ANSWER. THAT'S STRANGE.

HE DOESN'T HAVE MUCH TIME!

DING!

tick

ting

FROM G-DOG (GORDON)

FROM G-DOG (GORDON)

ALIEN ZAPPING PERIMETER

MEASURES HAVE BEEN TAKEN TO PROTECT P.U.R.S.T. HEADQUARTERS FROM FURTHER ATTACKS.

secret tunnel

sandbox entrance

force field radius

elevator

force field maker

Level one

Level two

NO ONE MESSES WITH
P.U.R.S.T.

NOT WHILE FLUFFY'S IN CHARGE.